THE CLASSIC COLLECTION OF SHORT STORIES

THIS TIME SOUMILI HAS COME UP WITH A SERIES OF CLASSIC INDIAN SHORT STORIES

SOUMILI PAUL

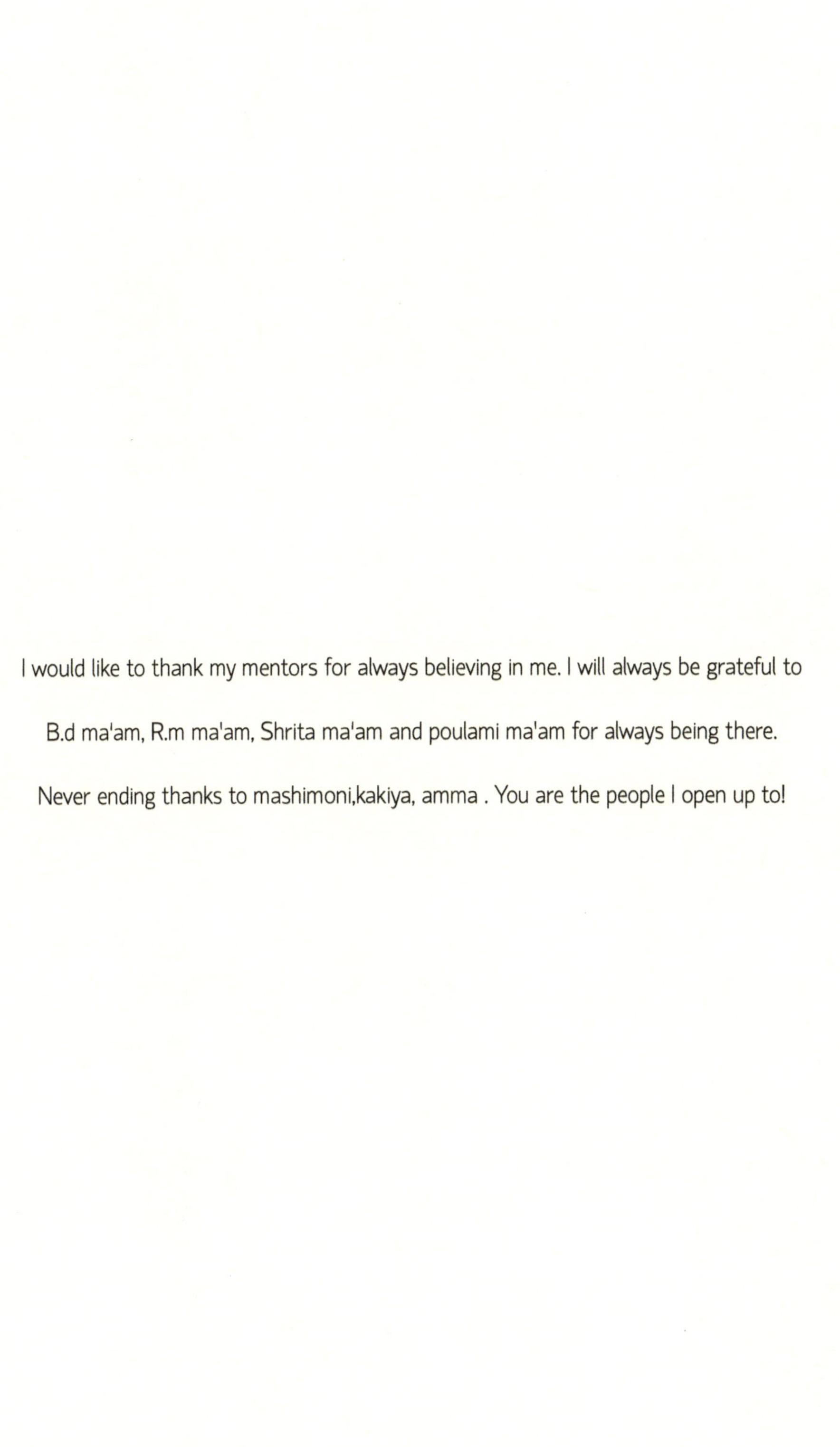

I would like to thank my mentors for always believing in me. I will always be grateful to

B.d ma'am, R.m ma'am, Shrita ma'am and poulami ma'am for always being there.

Never ending thanks to mashimoni,kakiya, amma . You are the people I open up to!

Contents

Acknowledgements

I would like to thank my husband for being my best friend and also worst enemy at times, I believe in god in every possible situation. I have always been backed up and restored by the both.

Even if metaphysically, stay forever.

CHAPTER ONE

POULAMI

POULAMI

Just as the name suggests she was also like a ray of the superfluous sun. She also had the very common nick name Polo as every girl named Poulami generally has. She is a professor, a professor who is as humble as dove. There was a lot of other students in her class who would chat with her, have fun in the class. None but one of her students managed to notice all of those which were not visible to others. She was a simple lady wearing no makeup and simple dresses to college. But her life achievements till date were as fine as her dupatta pleats. She had large eyes, pink absolutely pink lips that clearly says they are not known to any friend called lipstick. She was born to very simple parents who managed to brought up their daughter so well that she has never let them down even once. Abundant no. of students from small town dreams of becoming a government employee but women like Poulami doesn't really care about their luck nor opportunities they just go like the waves of a marine, confident and less bothered.

Poulami by now was the assistant professor of a government college in Kolkata. She was senior by designations to her elders in the college. Not sure if it ever came along her way as a delinquent but everything seemed perfect from the outer view. She had a really good batch as the seniors were far better than our batch then came the batch of 2019. A mixed batch of school love birds, college married couples and extreme studious to extreme wanderers. Not sure how was her experience with us! But if ever she was disturbed with something that would always be some of the college union members or our juniors both equally slighted her only then we would notice her eyes are pale her smile is not on its usual. Poulami was absolutely fond of plants, tiny little plants and seasonal flowers. Everyday she would put a status on her WhatsApp sharing the morning bliss of her life, the absolutely good looking balcony of her Kolkata flat continues to be on her story till date. Poulami had a wonder idea of arts, she would always help her dear students in arts and projects, sometimes I wondered she would also make it really well as art and craft teacher. I am a kind of person who always came in class with a lots of problem, I never ever felt that she got disturbed with any of my snags. Well, the fact that excited us the most was to see the pictures of her recent travel goals. At the last day of college, I was the most saddest person to leave the college. Those balconies, those dust in the library, those torn pages of the books really had my college days locked in there forever.

CHAPTER TWO

NIJU

THE STORY BEGINS FROM THE EARLY YEARS OF THE 60'S WHEN NILANJANA (NIJU) WAS BORN. SHE WAS BORN IN A VILLAGE OF BONGAON (BANGLADESH BORDER). SHE WAS HER PARENTS SECOND DAUGHTER AND THIRD CHILD; SHE HAD 8 SIBLINGS. NIJU'S FATHER'S NAME WAS TRILOKESH AND HE WAS A FARMER, SO HE HAD A TOUGH LIFE AFTER A WHOLE DAY OF HARD WORK HE COULD BARELY BE SEEN GIVING COMPANY TO THE KIDS. HER MOTHER WAS NAINA DEVI WHO WAS A VERY DEDICATED HOUSE WIFE AND A SUPPORT SYSTEM TO HIS DAD. THE FAMILY WERE VERY PARTRIARCHAL BY NATURE.
BASICALLY, IN THESE KIND OF FAMILIES WHEN A WOMAN GETS PREGNANT EVERYBODY AROUND KEEPS TELLING HER THAT IT HAS TO BE A BOY, A BOY WILL MULTIPLE THE PRIDE OF THE FAMILY AFTERALL AND A GIRL WILL ONLY BRING UP MISERIES. IN THAT WAY NIJU'S MOTHER HAS ALSO BEING THE VICTIM OF SUCH UTTERANCE FOR ATLEAST MORE THAN 4 TIMES IN HER LIFE BUT SHE IS RELAXED AS SHE HAS BORE 3 HEALTHY SONS. ACCORDING TO NIJU, A COUPLE SHOULD BE VERY POSSESSIVE AND SENSITIVE ABOUT THEI DECITIONS OF PARENTHOOD. THOUGH SHE BELONGED TO SUCH AN ORTHODOX SOCIETY SHE HAD A MODERN OUTLOOK. HER MOTHER HAS BEEN PREGNANT FOR ATLEAST 15 TIMES AND HAS MANAGED TO GIVE HEALTHY BIRTH TO ONLY 9 CHILDREN. SEEING THE CONDITION OF HER MOTHERS HEALTH SHE USED TO SUFFER FROM OVER-THINKING AND ANXIETY. WELL, SHE WAS ADMITTED TO A SCHOOL ONLY TILL HER 4TH STANDARD. AFTER THAT LOCALITY PEOPLE ADVISED HER FATHER TO MAKE HER SIT IN THE ROOM AND LEARN SOME HOUSEHOLD CHORES BECAUSE THAT IS ALL WHAT IS EXPECTED FROM HER.

WHEN SHE WAS TOLD TO DISCONTINUE THE SCHOOL, SHE WAS VERY HAPPY OF GETTING RID OF THE POSSIBILITY OF STUDYING. BUT WITHIN FEW MONTHS SHE UNDERTOOD THAT SHE WILL BE LIKE THIS ALL HER LIFE DEPENDING ON HER PARENTS AND WHATEVER BAD OR WORST THEY DECIDE FOR HER. LIMITATIONS ON GOING OUT AND PLAYING STARTED TO POP OUT ONCE SHE REACH THE AGE OF 11. SHE WAS ONLY ALLOWED TO PLAY WITH GIRLS AT THE BACKYARD. THE KIND OF LIFE SHE HAS BEEN SEEN TILL NOW IS LIKE MOTHER WAKES UP EARLY DOES ALL THE WORK. ANYTHING ANYWHERE GOES WRONG HER MOTHER IS BLAMED. HER FATHER AND BROTHERS ENJOY A SUPREME POSITION IN THE FAMILY WHAT EVER THEY NEED IS DONE BY EITHER THE MOTHER OR SISTERS. WIVES HERE ARE EXOECTED TO COOK, CLEAN, LOOK AFTER THE BABY AND ALSO HELP THEIR HUSBAND IN FARMING.

FEW YEARS PASSED LIKE THESE, WHEN NIJU TURNED 14 SOMETHING HAPPENED ON HER BIRTHDAY. HER MOTHER COOKED DELICIOUS MUTTON CURRY, ONION RINGS AND STEAMED RICE WITH BUTTER. SHE WAS COOKING SOME MORE ITEMS THAT NIJU REALLY LIKES BUT SUDDENLY NIJU'S GRANDMA, FATHER CAME IN THE KITCHEN KICKED THE CHULHA AND FEW DISHES WERE ABSOLUTELY SHATTERED AROUND THE KITCHEN FLOOR. NIJU'S MOTHER GOT BEATEN UP BY HER FATHER VERY BADLY. WITHOUT EVEN KNOWING ANYTHING SHE PLEADED FOR HIM TO RELEASE HER. NIJU STARTED TO CRY ALOUD THEN REST OF THE FAMILY RELAXED THE SITUATION. AFTER A WHILE N IJU CAME TO KNOW WHAT HAS HAPPENED! NIJU'S ELDER SISTER MONIKA WAS RETURNING FROM THE MARKET AND WAS STOPPED BY A STRANGER (YOUNG MAN), WHO WAS ASKING FOR SOME DIRECTIONS. THIS WAS SEEN BY SOME OF THE GRAM PANCHAYAT MEMBERS WHO DECIDED TO INFORM HER DAD ABOUT THIS AND TO MARRY HER OFF IMMEDIATELY BECAUSE SHE IS SHAMELESS, SHE CAN DO ANYTHING THAT CAN BE DISRESPECTFULL FOR THE VILLAGE. THE WEDDING TOOK PLACE IN JUST 2 DAYS WITH A KOLKATA BASED BUSINESS MAN. THE DAY OF VIDAY THE HOUSE WAS LEFT ONLY WITH MONIKA'S CLOTHES AND REMINISCENES. THAT NIGHT NIJU THOUGHT THAT WHAT COULD SHE DO TO AVOID SUCH SITUATION? SHE DECIDED ON HERSELF SHE WOULD

COMPLETELY RUN AWAY FROM ANY GUY ASKING ANYTHING TO HER.

3 MONTHS PASSEED, ON ONE EVE THE NEWS SURFACED THROUGH THE HOUSE THAT MONIKA IS NOT AT ALL HAPPY WITH HER MARRIAGE AND HAD A MISCARRIAGE AND STILL HER IN-LAWS ARE NOT ALLOWING HER TO VISIT HER PARENTAL HOUSE. NIJU STRESSED ON THIS AS SHE MISSES HER SISTER VERY MUCH. NIJU'S MOM TOLD HER TO FOCUS ON HER SKIN CARE AND HAIRCARE AS BOY'S FAMILY WILL START TO VISIT THEM WITHIN A WEEK.

THE FIRST ONE SAID YES TO NIJU AND WHY NOT BECAUSE SHE WAS ABSOLUTELY BEAUTIFUL WAIST LENGTH BLACK HAIR, FAIR COMPLEXION BIG SHINNING EYES WITH AN INNOCENT SMILE, SHE WAS AN EASY EXAMPLE OF BONG BEAUTY. THE MARRIAGE TOOK PLACE WITHIN 5 DAYS. THE FAMILY WERE IN A RUSH AS THE GROOM WILL TAKE NIJU TO BANGLADESH. THE MARRIAGE WENT WELL. GREAT ADVICE WERE GIVEN TO NIJU ABOUT PLEASING HIS HUSBAND ON THE WEDDING NIGHT. THE WEDDING NIGHT ARRIVED AND THAT IS WHEN SHE REALISED THAT THINGS DID NOT WATCH HOW SHE WAS TOLD IT WOULD SHE FELT LIKE A BIRD TRAPPED IN A NEST.

SHE TRIED TO SCREAM AND CRY ALOUD BUT THERE WAS NO HOPE. AT DAWN, SHE DICOVERED THAT HE HAS BLEEDED SO THE BEDSHEET IS STAINED. NIJU GETS VERY SCARED AS SHE DOESN'T KNOW ANYTHING ABOUT THE NEW HOUSE AND IT'S WHEREABOUTS. NIJU FINALLY GATHERS THE COURAGE TO CALL HER HUSBAND AND INFORM HIM THE SITUATION. BUT THE HUSBAND CALLED THIS DISTURBING AS TO WHY DID SHE RUIN HIS SLEEP OVER THIS. SHE THEN SOMEHOW MANAGES TROUBLES ONE AFTER THE OTHER BY HER OWN AND HE KEPT ON PRAYING TO GOD, CHANTING RADHEGOBINDO JUST AS HER MOTHER WOULD DO. SHE TOOK BATH IN A PARTITIONED ROOM WITHOUT ROOF, THE KIND OF BATHROOM THEY HAD. SHE TOUCHED HERSELF AS SHE FELT THE BODYACHE, SHE FELT LIKE A FLOWER WHO'S CHASTITY AND PURITY HAS BEEN ABOLISHED. NIJU SUFFERED A LOT IN HIS IN-LAWS HOUSE. RANDOMNLY, SHE GOT BITTEN-UP FROM HER HUSBAND AND MOTHER-IN-LAW. LIFE BECAME A LIVING HELL FOR HER. SHE COULDN'T BEAR IT WHEN

HER MOTHER-IN-LAW ALWAYS TRICKED TO MAKE HER THE CULPRIT FOR EVERYTHING. SURPRISINGLY ONE DAY SHE GETS REALLY BITTEN-UP BADLY BY HER HUSBAND AS HE DISCOVERS SHE IS NOT A 10TH PASS. THIS CONTINUED FOR SOME MORE MONTHS BECAUSE OF LACKING IN PROPER NUTRITION SHE STARTED TO LOSE WEIGHT AND LOOK SICK AND TIRED. THE DAY OF JOY CAME IN HER LIFE WHEN SHE DISCOVERS THAT SHE IS PREGNANT! THIS WAS HER BEST CHANCE TO VISIT HER PARENTAL HOME, NIJU WAS DYING TO SEE HER PARENTS.

SWHE FINALLY GOT HOME AND EMBRACED HER MOTHER, AFTER A WHILE SHE REALIZES THAT HER PARENTS ARE TENSED ABOUT SOMETHING. AFTER NIJU REPEATEDLY ASKED THEM WHAT WAS WRONG THEY SAID HER IN-LAWS HAS DEMANDED 200 GRAMS OF GOLD IF SHE IS UNABLE TO BEAR A BOY CHILD, NIJU HAS BEEN ASKED NOT TO RETURN IN HER IN-LAWS UNTIL SHE DELIVERS!

THIS WAS THE FIRST TIME IN NIJU'S LIFE THAT SHE FELT SHE WAS NOT ATALL WELCOMED IN HER OWN HOME. HER GRANDMA STARTED TO SAY THINGS LIKE WHY WOULD YOU WANT TO VISIT US? YOU ARE THE REASON OF THEIR DISTURBED MIND AND NATURE. HELPLESS NIJU LOOKED AT HER MOTHER BUT EVEN HER MOTHER DID NOT TAKE ANY STAND FOR HER, SHE ALSO BHAD HEADACHES ABOUT THE OTHER TWO DAUGHTER'S MARRIAGE AND THEIR DOWRY!

THE 15 YEAR OLD COULDN'T UNDERSTAND WHAT IS GOING ON IN HER LIFE! SHE SPENDED MOST OF HER TIMES CHANTING PRAYERS, DOING LIGHT HOUSEHOLD WORKS AND SPENDING TIME WITH HER SIBLINGS. FINALLY, THE DAY COMES AND SHE DELIVERS HER BABY BOY. SHE WAS SO HAPPY TO HOLD HER BABY FOR THE VERY FIRST TIME, BUT SHE HAD A C-SECTION DELIVERY DUE TO SOME COMPLICATIONS. THE NEWS SURFACED AND PEOPLE STARTED TO COMMENT ON HER DELIVERY SAYING: 'THIS WAS An EASY WAY TO GIVE BIRTH, SHE DIDN'T EVEN BEAR THE LABOUR THEN HOW CAN SHE BE A GOOD MOTHER, SHE JUST ENTERENED MOTHERHOOD JUST LIKE THAT!'

ALL THESE TORTURED NIJU, SHE COULDN'T IGNORE ALL OF THEM. SHE RETURNED TO HER IN-LAWS. SHE FELT THEY WERE HAPPY ABOUT THE BABY BOY. BUT, AS THE DAYS PASSED OLD

TOTURES BEGAN A ND SHE COULDN'T EVEN PROPERLY FEED HER BABY, THE BABY TURNED OUT TO BE VERY GOOD LIKE, JUST LIKE HER MOTHER BUT NIJU COULDN'T PROVIDE EVEN EDUCATION TO HIM. SHDE GAVE UP ON LIFE. DAYS WOULD PASS SHE WONT COOK AS THERE WOULD BE ONLY STEAM RICE TO RICE OR PUFFED RICE, NOT EVEN POTATO OR LENTIL. SHE SAW HOW HER IN-LAWS SEPARETED THEM IN OUTHOUSE AND THEY LIVED IN SUCH HARMONY. A WOMAN STARTED VISITING THEIR HOME WITH NIJU'S HUSBAND. NIJU DOUBTED THAT TWO ARE IN A RELATIONSHIP. SHE NAMED HER SON LAKSYA, SHE WAS SURPRISED TO SEE THAT HER IN -LAWS DIDN'T EVEN LOVED LAKSYA. LAKSYA WAS ADORED BY THEIR VILLAGE PEOPLE THEIR HOUSE WAS ON RIVER-SIDE AT BANGLADESH.

OFTEN THEIR NEIGHBOUR WOULD ASK LAKSYA WHAT DID YOU HAVE IN LUNCH? AND THE BABY BOY WITHOUT KNOWING THE CRUELTY OF REALITY WOULD REPLY IN INNOCENSE SAYING MY MOTHER DIDN'T COOK TODAY! EVERYDAY SOMEONE FROM THE NEIGHBOURHOOD WOULD FEED LAKSYA. ONE DAY, NIJU'S FATHER TRILOKESH ALONG WITH HER BIG BROTHER NIKHILESH (NIKHIL) WOULD VISIT HER HOUSE TO CHECK ON HER AND BROUGHT A BAG FULL OF SEASONAL FRUIT MANGO A BIG HILSA FISH AND SWEET CURD IN A RED EARTHEN POT AS OFFERING TO HER IN-LAWS. NIJU'S IN-LAWS WERE NOT PLEASED TO SEE HER PARENTS. NIJU BURST OUT INTO TEARS AND SAID EVERYTHING TO HER PARENTS REQUESTING THEM TO TAKE HER ALONG WITH THEM. NIJU'S FATHER ABOUT HER HUSBAND'S AFFAIR AS HE WAS WALKING IN THE HOUSE WITH HIS GIRLFRIEND WITHOUT KNOWING THAT HIS IN-LAWS ARE RIGHT PRESENT OVER THERE! THOUGH TRILOKESH WAS REALLY NOT INTERESTED IN TALKING BACK HIS DAUGHTER BUT LOOKING AT HIS GRANDCHILD'S FACE HE WAS CONFUSED. AT THIS POINT, NIKHIL TOOK A STAND FOR NILANJANA AND ASKED HIS FATHER TO TAKE NIJU BACK WITH THEM.

A YEAR PASSED AWAY, SHE WAS 17, HUSBAND-LESS, HAD AN ILLETERATE CHILD, BEING A BURDEN FOR THE FAMILY NIJU WENT INTO SERIOUS DEDPRESSION. MONTHS PASSED AND ONE DAY HER GRANDMA DIED. PATRIORCHAL RULES SEEMED TO BE RELAXED A BIT SINCE THEN. LAKSYA WAS ADMITTED TO SCHOOL BY NIKHIL.

NIJU REMAINED BUSY WITH OTHER HOUSE HOLD CHORES WITH HER MOTHER AS NONE OF HER BROTHERS WERE MARRIED BY THEN.

YEARS PASSED, ONE BY ONE HER BROTHERS GOT MARRIED. EVERYONE BEHAVED WITH HER IN A RUDE WAY. SHE WAS AS IF OF NO VALUE. WHEN LAKSYA GOT PROMOTED TGO CLASS 10 NIJU'S FAMILY DECIDED TO STOP LAKSYA FROM GOING TO SCHOOL AS THE EXPENSES OF THE FAMILY GOT VERY HIGH AFTER HER BROTHERS ALSO HAD CHILDREN. NIJU WAS UNDER SHOCK SHE THOUGHT FOR A MINUTE THAT THERE WAS NO WAY SHE COULD BEAR THE COST OF HIS STUDIES SHE DOESN'T HAVE AN SKILL TO WORK, DOESN'T HAVE ANY JEWELLARY TO SALE EITHER. SHE PLEADED TO HER MOTHER, REQUESTED HER BROTHER'S WIVES THAT SHE WOULD WORK HARD DO THEIR PART OF THE WORK AS WELL BUT JUST TO ATLEAST LET LAKSYA COMPLETE HIS 10TH. THEY AGREED, LAKSYA SECURED A GOOD MARKS AND SOON AFTER STARTED TO DO SOME FARMING JOBS FOR THE FAMILY. SUDDENLY, ONE DAY LAKSYA FATHER VIPIN VISITED THEIR HOME. BEING THE JAMAI, GROOMS ALWAYS ENJOYED A SENSE OF ATTENTION IN EVERY FAMILY NO MATTER WHAT. HE CONVINCED NIJU TO COME ALONG WITH HIM TO BRINDABAN WHERE HE HAS STARTED THE JOB OF A TOUR GUIDE. NIJU BID GOODBYE TO HER FAMILY AND WENT OFF TO BRINDABAN WITH SON AND HUSBAND.

AFTER 2 YEARS SHE REALIZED SHE HAS AGAIN BEEN FOOLED BY HER HUSBAND AS HE HAS LEFT BRINFABAN AND WENT TO BANGLADESH WITHOUT INFORMING HER. SHE REMAINED AS A MAID FOR TWO YEARS DOING ALL THE WORK AND LAKSYA WOULD ALSO WORK FOR PART-TIME JOBS TO SUPPORT THE FAMILY, QUITTING HIS STUDIES. THIS SMALL NUCLEAR FAMILY WAS LIKE A BLISS TO THEM.BUT, THEIR DREAM CAME OUT TO BE FALSE. DISHEARTEDNED THEY THOUGHT NOT TO RETURN TO BONGAON EITHER. MOTHER AND SON WHO HAS ALWAYS BEEN THE CENTRE OF HATRED AND DISRESPECT THOUGHT TO NOT BEG TO ANYONE THIS TIME. NOW THEBIG QUESTION WAS WHAT TO DO WHO WILL PAY THE RENT, BILLS EVERYTHING? THAT'S WHEN LAKSYA STARTED TO WORK DAYA ND NIGHT TO RUN THE FAMILY. NILANJANA ACCIDENTLY FELT VERY SICK HER RIGHT FOOT

SWELLED UP AND SHE PRACTICALLY COULDN'T DO ANYTHING. ALL THE HOUSEHOLD CHORES WERE MANAGED BY LAKSYA ITSELF. THIS WENT ON FOR SOME MORE MONTHS AND LAKSYA FELT SICK SEVERELY. THEY RETUJRNED TO BONGAON, SAME OLD LIFE, LAKSYA STARTED TO WORK ON FIELDS. NIJU REMAINED BUSY COOKING, WASHING AND CLEANING. VIPIN STARTED TO VISIT THEM OFTEN EVERYTIME IN NEW ATTIRE AS A COSTUME SHOW. NIJU'S FAMILY REPEATEDLY ASKED VIPIN TO TAKE NILANJANA ALONG WITH HIM TO BANGLADESH BUT HE REFUSED. AT THIS POINT, NILANJANA THOUGH AWARE OF THE SITUATION TRIED NOT TO TRUST HIM AGAIN BUT ENDED UP AGAIN DREAMING OF A NORMAL FAMILY. THIS WAS GOING QUITE WELL ONLY WHEN VIPIN AGAIN VANISHED. THE GOT TO KNOWS GTHE MAN WAS A COMPLETE FRAUD RENTED FROM MANY PLACES AND HAS FINALLY FLEED AWAY TO BANGLADESH. NIJU DEEP DOWN JUST FELT THAT VIPIN LOVES HIM, WHAT COULD SHE ANYWAYS THINK? AFTERALL VIPIN IS THE ONLY PERSON SHE HAS LOVED ALL HER LIFE.

ON ONE FINE EVE VIPIN CALLS ON THEIR LANDLINE NO. AND SAYS THAT HE HAS MARRIED ANOTHER GIRL AND HAS STARTED A NEW LIFE. NIJU BREAKED IN TO PIECES AFTER THIS. NIKHIL BRINGS NIJU AND LAKSYA TO KOLKATTA HELPS LAKSYA TO RUN HIS BUSINESS AS A STARTUP AND HELP THEM TO GET A SMALL RENTED FLAT. NIJU WAS NOW ON HER EARLY 40'S , SHE NOW DREAMT OF JUST A NORMAL FAMILY WITH SON , DAUGHTER-IN-LAW AND GRANDCHILDREN. BUT, SOON SHED FACED THE REALITY HER SON LAKSYA WHO HAPPENED TO BE SO NICE HAS CHANGED A LOT! HE NOW WANTED TO GET RID OF HIS MOTHER AND SEE SEVERAL GIRFLS BRIN G THEM ON FLAT AND ENJOY HIS LIFE. SOON AFTER HIS MOTHER NIJU SENSED HIS INTENTIONS SHE FORCED HIM TO GET MARRIED. LAKSYA HAD A GIRLFRIEND CALLED RUPA. THEY GOT MARRIED SECRETLY WITHOUT INFORMING THE WHOLE FAMILY, TOOK AWAY ALL OF NIJU'S GOLDS AND ASKED HER TO GO B ACK TO BONGAON. NIJU PRFOTESTED BUT ALL HER EFFORT WENT IN TO VAIN AND SOON SHE WAS SENT BACK TO BONGAON. WHILE SHE RETURNED TO HER HOME THIS TIME HER POSITION WAS WAY WORST THAN EVER AS SHE EARNED THE TAG OF A BAD MOTHER-IN-LAW TOO.

PEOPLE STARTED TO JUDGE HER SAYING THINGS LIKE NEITHER WITH HUSBAND NOR WITH SON SHE COULD ADJUST. NILANJANA WAS NOW FACING DEPRESSION AND SHE PRACTICALLY STOPPED DOING ALL THE POSITIVE THINGS IN HER LIFE. SOON AFTER, SHE GOT THE NEWS THAT SHE WAS A GRANDMOTHER NOW AS HER DAUGHER-IN-LAW GAVE BIRTH TO A BABY GIRL, DESPITE THE BITTER RELATION NIJU CONGRATULATED RUPA. RUPA IN RETURN INSULTED HER BY SAYING NIJU COULDN'T UPBRING HER SON WELL, RUPA COMPLINED THAT WHILE SHE WAS PREGNANT LAKSYA WAS DATING OTHER GIRLS. EVERY TIME SHE CAUGHTS HIM RED-HANDED. HEARING ALL THESE DEEP DOWN, NIJU KNEW THAT RUPA WAS NOT LYING, SHE FELT BAD ABOUT RUPA AS LAKSYA HAS STARTED ACTING LIKE HIS DAD. NILANJANA ASKED RUPA THAT I AM MILES AWAY HERE, WHAT CAN I DO ABOUT THE SITUATION? I AM THAT UNFORTUNATE LADY WHO IS BEEN KICKED OUT BY HER OWN SON. YOU ARE HIS WIFE, HIS SOUL-MATE.THEN STOP THINKING ABOUT GIVING UP AND TRY TO MAKE MY SON A BETTER PERSON FOR YOU.

THIS CONTINUED FOR MORE THAN 3 YEARS. SOMETIMES RUPA MIGHT CALL NILANJANA TO SHOUT AND ARGUE AN D SOMETIMES LAKSYA CALLED TO TALK ABOUT LENDING MONEY AND PROPERTY. UNTIL ONE DAY WHEN IN 3 YEARS LAKSYA CAME TO VISIT NIJU TO INFORM THAT HE HAD A DIVORCE. HE APOLOGIZED TO HIS MOTHER. LAKSYA BROUGHT HIS MOTHER BACK TOOK A NEW RENTAL APARTMENT AND STARTING LIVING THERE. NIJU DISCOVERED THAT LAKSYA HAS GROWN HIS BUSINESS REALLY BIG BUT HAS DEVELOPED VERY BITTER RELATION WITH NIKHILESH AND FEW OTHERS OF THEIR FAMILY.

NIJU NEVER BROUGHT BACK ANY OLD TOPIC AS SHE WANTED HIM TO MOVE ON AND LEAD A BETTER LIFE. SOME TIMES TOXIC PEOPLE AROUND THEM WOULD TAUNT LAKSYA BUT NIJU ALWAYS ACTED WITH PATIENCE AND NEVER REACTED. 9 MONTHS PASSED LIKE THIS ONLY WHEN NIJU ONCE REALIZED THAT ALL HER DOCUMENTS, ADDRESS PROOF AND IDENTITY DOCUMENTS ALL ARE GONE. SHE WAITED FOR LAKSYA TO RETURN FROM WORK. LAKSYA RETURNED FROM HOME AROUND 9 AT NIGHT. NIJU ASKED HIM ABOUT THE DOCUMENTS. LAKSYA THOUGHT FOR A MOMENT AND SAID THAT I CANNOT D=FIND MY FOUR-WHEELER

DOCUMENTS AND LICENCE TOO. LET ME CALL RUPA AND ASK!
LATER THE NEXT DAY MORNING, LAKSYA INFORMS HIS MOTHER
THAT SHE HAS INTENTIONALLY TAKEN AWAY ALL THE PAPERS.
SHE IS ASKING LAKSYA TO PAY OFF THE ALIMONY OUT OF COURT.
LAKSYA ASKED NIJU TO WAIT FOR SOME MORE DAYS.
DAYS PASSEED AND THINGS WENT ON LIKE THE SAME. THEIR
2BHK APARTMENT WAS GRTTING FILLED WITH SECOND HAND
FURNITURES AND LAKSYA ALSO BOUGHT MICROWAVE AND
REFRIGARETOR FOR THE KITCHEN. THEY NOW HAD A 32 INCH
SMART TV IN THEIR LIVING CUM DINNING ROOM.
NIJU WOULD SPENT ALL HER TIME READING THE HOLY BOOKS,
COOKING DISHES, CLEANING HOUSE, WATCHING TV AND
WASHING ENDLESS CLOTHES.
YES, WASHING ENDLESS CLOTHES BECAUSE THEY ALSO HAD A
PART BUSINESS OF DRY CLEANING. SO YES, THOSE CLOTHES WERE
WASHED AT HOME USING SOME CHEMICALS. THIS WENT ON FOR
ANOTHER 2 YEARS. THEN NILANJANA SUFFERED WITH HER HAND
AS THE SKIN STARTED REACTING BECAUSE OF THE CHEMICALS.
SHE CONSUKTED DOCTOR AND WAS ASKED TO TAKE FULL BED
REST. THAT BIS WHEN IT STRIKED LAKSYA THAT HE SHOULD
HAVE THOUGHT ABOUT A DOMESTIC HELP EARLIER. HE QUICKLY
ASSIGNED A PERSON WHO'S NAME WAS PARUL TO HELP HIS MA.
PARUL DID ALL THE HOUSEHOLD WORKS. PARUL WAS THE SAME
AGE AS WAS LAKYSA. SOMETIMES SHE WOULD WATCH A WEB
SERIIES WITH NIJU OR HEAR STORIES ABOUT NIJU'S PAST LIFE.
NIJU GRADUALLY GOT BETTER AND RETURNED TO HER FORM BUT
THE CHEMICAL WASHING WAS STOPPED FOR HER. LAKSYA
APPOINTED TWO MORE BOYS FOR THE TASK.
SEEING LAKSYA SOMETIMES NIJU FELT VERY GOOD. MOTHER
AND SON SAW A LOT IN LIFE BUT FINALLY THEY ARE HAVING A
PEACEFUL LIFE! IN THE MONTH OF JANUARY,2018 THEY WERE
INVITED FOR NIKHILESH'S ELDER SON'S MARRIAGE. SHE WAS
REALLY HAPPY
TO REUNITE WITH THE FAMILY BUT HAD NO IDEA ON WHAT
SHE SHOULD GIFT TO NIKHILESH'S DAUGHTER IN LAW. SHE THEN
QUICKLY TOOK OUT THE ONLY PAIR OF GOLD BANGLES SHE WAS
LEFT WITH, SHE LOOKED AT THEM VERY CAREFULLY AND ASKED
LAKSYA TO TAKE THEM FOR POLISHING. LAKSYA PROTESTED

SEEEING THIS, HE SAID I CANNOT AFFORD GIVING GOLD PRESENT TO THEM MA! AND YOU ARE ONLY LEFT WITH THIS WHAT WILL YOU GIVE WHEN REST OF THE BROTHERS WILL GET MARRIED. NIJU FALLED SILENT. LAKSYA THEN SUGGESTED HIS MOM TO BUY A GOOD SAREE FOR THE BRIDE.

THEN, AFTER FEW DAYS THE MARRIAGE TOOK PLACE AND NIJU WAS REUNITED WITH HER FAMILY. SHE WAS VERY HAPPY TO BE AROUND HER FAMILY.

2020 MARCH, THE MONTH PANDEMIC BREAKED OUT IN KOLKATA. IT GOT REALLY WORST FOR ALL! LAKSYA'S IRON BUSINESS AND DRY-CLEANING BUSINESS GOT SHUT. HE NOW ONLY RELIED ON WATER SUPPLY AND RAPIDO. YES, RAPIDO IS THE BIKE-TAXI APP. NILANJANA WOULD SPEND HER DAYS IN MISERY THINKING ABOUT LAKSYA AS HE RIDED HIS BIKE DAY AND NIGHT WITHOUT LICENSE AND PROPER SAFETY. TWICE HE HAS FACED ACCIDENT. NILANJANA DISCOVERED THAT THE URGE OF INCOMING SO MUCH OF MOEY IS NOT BECAUSE OF RUNNING THIS HOUSE BUT TO RUN ANOTHER HOUSE THAT HE HAS DEVELOPED FOR HIM. HE ALSO WAS STAYING IN A LIVING RELATION WITH A GIRL 2 YEARS ELDER THAN HIS AGE HAVING 3 CHILDREN. THE WOMAN'S NAME WAS PARUL! THE DOMESTIC HELPING MAID OF THEIR HOUSE. NILANJANA GOT TO KNOW ALL THESE FROM THE LITTLE HELPING BOY OF LAKSYA'S WATER SUPPLYING BUSINESS. SHE CALLED UP LAKSYA AND SAID A LOT OF BITTER WORDS EXPRESSING ALL HER WORRIES AND FRUSTRATION.

IT WAS NOT TOO LATE AFTER THIS THAT LAKSYA COMPLETELY STOPPED VISITING HIS MA, EVEN STOPPED BUYING NECESITIES FOR HER. SHE RUN OUT OF MEDICINE AND FOOD. SOMETIMES LAKYA WOULD SEND HER BACK TO BONGAON BUT, EVEN THERE PEOPLE WERE IRRITATED TO SEE HER AND LOOK AFTER HER. SHE IN HER KOLKATA FLAT WOULD REMAIN HUNGRY FOR DAYS WAITING FOR LAKSYA TO COME. SOMETIMES SHE CALLED UP SOME OF HER WELL WISHERS IN THE FAMILY TO CALL UP LAKSYA AND ASK HIM TO GET HER SOME GROCERIES. THINGS WENT WORST WHEN THE FLAT WHERE SHE WAS LIVING IN, THE LAND LADY ASKED HER TO LEAVE THE APARTMENT AS SHE WISHED TO SALE IT. SHE HAD NO BALANCE IN HER MOBILE PHONE SO SHE KEPT ON GIVING MIST CALLS TO LAKSYA UNTIL HE CALLED BACK.

HEAFRING EVERYTHING LAKSYA SAID THAT FINE YOU COME IN OUR APARTMENT AND STAY WITH US. NILANJANA REPLIED IN IRRITATION THAT IF IT WAS HIS MARRIED WIFE SHE WOULD HAVE COME ALONG BUT SHE WAS A MAID WITH CHILDREN HE WAS LIVING WITH. THE FINAL DAY ARRIVED WHEN SHE WAS ASKED TO LEAVE THE FLAT. FOR THE LAST TIME SHE CALLED UP NIKHILESH ONLY THAT LAKSYA TOOK PARUL TO SEVERAL PLACES AND WAS UNDER THE RAID OF THE POILCE EVERYTIME HE ESPACED USING NIKHILESH'S NAME. THEY WERE MAD AT NIJU AND HER SON. SHE CALLED AT BONGAON TO KNOW LAKSYA ALSO HAS SEVERAL RELATIONS WITH SOME GIRLS THERE AND HAS ALSO SLEPT WITH THEM. LAKSYA WAS FULLY SCANDALIZED OVER THERE.

NILANJANA WENT SILENT FOR 5 MINS, SHE SAT ON A SOFA PRACTICALLY DOING NOTHING. SHE DRANK SOME OF THE WATER FROM THE BOTTLE BESIDE HER BED AND DECIDED ON DOING SOMETHING COMPLETE DIFFERENT FROM HER PERSONALITY. SHE TOOK OUT THOSE TWO BANGLES WENT TO THE JEWELLARY SHOP TO SELL THEM. SHE GOT 70,000 SELLING THEM. SHE CAME BACK TOOK 5 THOUSAND AND WENT TO THE LAND LADY ASKED HER TO CONSIDER HER FOR 15 MORE DAYS IN RETUR SHE WOULD PAY DOUBLE THE RENT. THE LAND LADY THOUGHT FOR A MOMENT AND AGREED TO HER PROPOSAL.IN THE EVENING SHE WENT OUT TO THE LOCAL MARKET PURCHASED 5 UNIFORM SAREES AND BOUGHT SOME GROCERIES. LATER THAT NIGHT AFTER HAVING DINNER SHE THOUGHT ABOUT HER PLANS THE NEXT DAY AND WENT OFF TO SLEEP PEACEFULLY. THE VERY NEXT DAY SHE PLANNED TO VISIT URBANNA A BIG HOUSING NEXT TO HER FLAT TO TALK WITH THEM REGARDING COOKING WORK, BUT SHE NEEDED AN ACCESS TO GET UP. SO, SHE USED HER CONTACT SUDIPA A WOMAN OF HER AGE SHE KNEW FROM THE LOCALITY. SHE CALLED UP SUDIPA AND ASKED IF SHE CAN COME OVER. SUDIPA THOUGH FELT AWKARD BUT STILL SAID YES. REACHING THERE SHE CAME TO KNOW THAT SUDIPA DOES ALL HER CHORES ALONE AS DOCTOR HAS SUGEESTED HER TO HVE A LOT OF PHYSICAL ACTIVITIES. BUT, SHE SAID NIJU THAT I CAN CHECK WITH MY SON AND DAUGHTER-IN-LAW AS THEY ARE BOTH WORKING PROFFESIONALS THEY NEEDS DOMESTIC HELP VERY

BADLY. AS ALL THE MAIDS ARE GONE FOR THIS LOCKDOWN. WITHIN AN HOUR EVERYTHING WAS SET.

SUDIPA'S SON AND DAUGHTER-IN-LAW WERE EDITORS AND SUPER BUSY WORKING COUPLE AMAYRA AND AKASH DIDN'T HAVE ANY CHILD AND WAS LOOKING FOR A LADY WHO WOULD ALL THE CHORES STAYING WITH THEM IN THE MAID'S ROOM. NIJU AGREED TO EVERYTHING THEY OFFEREDC HER A SALARY OF 12 THOUSAND. NILANJANA COULDN'T BELIEVE HER EARS. SHE WENT BACK TO HER APARTMENT PACKED HER CLOTHES IN A SUITCASE TOOK HERS GODS HOME TEMPLE AND HOLY BOOKS IN ANOTHER SUITCADSE AND LEFT THE FLAT. SHE MOVED IN URBANNA. SHE CALLED UP LAKSYA JUST TO INFORM THAT HE CAN TAKE AWAY ALL THE FURNITURES AND ELECTRICAL APPLIANCES IF HE WANTED TO. THAT WAS THE LAST YTIME SHE SPOKE TO LAKSYA. SHE BREAKED HER SIM CARD AND THREWB INTO TRASH. WITHING FEW DAYS SHE GOT A NEW SIM CARD AND OPENED A BANK ACCOUNT TO DEPOSIT HER CASH . WITHIN ONE MONTH, SHE BOUGHT AN ANDROID PHONE SO THAT SHE CAN LISTEN TO HOLY SONGS WHILE DOING WORKS. ONE DAY SHE WAS RETURNING FROM THE MARKET AND SHE NOTICED HERSELF IN THE LIFT MIRROR AND WAS AMAZED AT THE BEAUTY OF HER THIS NEW LIFE, NOT DEPENDING UPON ANYONE, NOT BOWING TO ANYONE SHE FELT SHE WAS REBORN. SHE ALWAYS CHANTED PRAYERS AND THANKED HER SEVERAL GODS FOR GIVING HER SO MUCH OF STRENGH. SHE DIDN'T LOOK BACK AT HER FAMILY TILL DATE AS SHE KNEW THE KIND OF PATRIORCHAL FAMILY SHE CAME FROM WOULD NEVER ACCEPT HER NEW NEW LIFE. SHE CONTINUED TO WORK THER AFTER 3 MONTHS OF JOINING HERE SHE BOUGHT A STICHING MACHINE AND STARTED TO STITCH FOR THE HOUSING PEOPLE AND MAKE A GOOD AMOUNT OF EXTRA MONEY IN A MONTH.

ONCE AMAYRA ASKED HER THAY WHERE DID SHE LEARNED STICHING FROM NIJU SMILED AND SAID YOUTUBE. AMAYRA AND AKSASH WOULD ALWAYS SUPPORT HER AS SHE DID ALL THE CHORES OF THE HOUSEHOLD SINGLE-HANDEDLY AND STILL MANAGED TO OVER-WORK. AT THE END OF THE YEAR 2021, SHE LEFT URBANNA AND SHIFTED TO A 2BHK RENTED APARTMENT AT A NEARBY LOCATION AND STARTED HER NEW BUSINESS OF A

CLOUD KITCHEN. SHE STILL CONTINUED TO WORK FOR AMAYRA
ONLY FOR THE COOKING PART. AS THEY GAVE BIRTH TO A
BEAUTIFUL DAUGHTER AND THEY NEEDED A 24/7 BABY SITTER
BUT THEY CAN'T THINK OF HAVING FOOD ANYWHERE ELSE.
NILANJANA NOW HANDLES HER CLOUD KITCKEN, TAILORING
BUSINEES AND COOKING JOB ALL TOGETHER. AS MUCH AS I HAVE
SEEN IN MY LIFE SHE IS THE MOST STRONG SINGLE
MULTI-TASTKING FEARLESS WOMAN I HAVE EVER MET.
THIS IS NOT A FICTIONAL STORY, THEN WHO AM I?
I AM HER NEIGHBOUR, JUST THOUGHT TO PEN DOWN HER
LIFESTORY, LEAVING THE REST UPTO MY READERS.
SOUMILI PAUL.

CHAPTER THREE

SHINJINI

The story revolves around a Bengali lower middle-class girl, a young little baby girl. Whenever we say little girl we tend to create an image in our mind of the girl by thinking what the girl might look like! Maybe the girl has got waist length hair maybe not, an innocent face, pretty eyes. Yes, the girl I am talking about had all of the above features. Her name was Shinjini she also had a nick name and that is Dodo. Bongs always carry a nickname(daknam) along with their valo naam (official name).

So, Shinjini was an average girl, average in studies, average in extra-curriculum activities and also average by looks till her 14th birthday. Dodo was quantity over quality kind of a girl. She was into atleast 5 types of extra-curriculum activities. She was always praised by others for her flawless dance and sports.

Shinjini lived with her mother, her father passed away when he was 3 years old. Her mother's name was Tanushree, she worked for a private bank. Her salary was somewhere between 20-25k but she had to pay off 80% of her salary for the home loan EMI's and her husband Subho's personal loan interests. The rest of the money was not enough to pay for Shinjini's education and to run all the costs of the household bills. Tanushree's life was a living hell according to her, only thing which made her happy was Shinjini. The only precious gift that her husband left for her. But, somehow in life we forget to give importance and love to our most loved one's under the pressure of situation. Same thing happened to Tanushree as well, under the backpack of loans, EMI's, personal life emptiness she forgot to connect with her daughter through all the passing years. Both mother and daughter were very fast-forward in terms of decision making.

Subho and Tanushree got married in the year 1998 and bought a beautiful 2bhk flat at Dhakuria, south Kolkata. But, Subho unfortunately couldn't walk the alley of a marriage or fatherhood for a long time! He got lungs cancer and bid goodbye to his family when Shinjini was just 3 years and one month old. Tanushree actually was suggested by a lot of people to get married once again, she even dated few people till she was 40 but none worked out for her as no one was ready to accept her daughter Shinjini alongside. Shinjini knew all these, she has always been a great support to her mother. Shinjini knew the financial status of the family and thus was very eager to earn money from a very young age. she had all her plans set post 10th. Shinjini went to a girls school, all her coaching classes contained more girls than boys only if there was a prospect she would only find one or two studs scholar looking boys who always glared at their text books and didn't know much about the outside world. Shinjini's world was with her mom and her school friends she barely had any relatives from his father's side as her father's family considered her mother to be an evil wife because her father was suffering with health problem from right after his marriage.

December,2011.

On one fine morning, Shinjini asked Tanushree whether she can join the new yoga class that was going to start in her school. Tanushree looked aghast. Tanushree cleared her throat before speaking, she looked straight at Dodo's eyes and said I wanted to talk to you about this. By then Dodo stopped browsing and observed at her mom, her mom continued to speak she said I want to cut some cost on our living by now as you will be promoted to class 9 next year and I need to provide you with at least few more tutors till 10th. Tanushree didn't cared about her daughter's extra curriculum goings-on because she knew what was more important. Dodo agreed and said so what else do you want me to cut on? Shall I stop basket ball and drawing classes too? Tanushree said no for now, anyway you have few more months to do all these then for two years only books will be your life . Dodo whispered do I need to stop my dance as well? Her mother though busy finding her wrist watch as she is rushing to office replied her with a smile no, you don't need to stop that only if you manage to get 75% marks in your mini madhyamik. Dodo replied deal!

Dodo for the next two months was busy doing her classes, extra curriculum activities and the thing she loved the most was to spend time talking to friends over phone (not in person). She hated watching tv the most. Dodo used to attend her morning school, she was in an elite private English medium school and all her friend circle included friends from well to do families. She came back home around 6 doing her tuitions and after school activities and her home tutors visited around 8:30 and leave by 10. By

11 she would be at her bed. Tanushree on the other hand did all the chores of the house hold and left the house by 9 and would return around 8. Sunday was Tanushree's only off day which she would spend buying groceries for the week pay bills and relax the rest half watching a movie with Dodo or just visit her side of the relatives. Dodo and Tanushree's relation was fine until Dodo was too young but gradually by the passing years things have been so straight-forward in their relation. They were way too predictable to each other. Tanushree was suffering from mental illness she didn't care much about her looks or life anymore she would always feel very frustrated with her life. She much elder than her age. Unfortunately, none of these were noticed by Dodo.

May, 2012.

Tanushree and Dodo were having dinner around 10 passed 10 both were inaudible when suddenly Dodo came up with an idea of going to shopping at Havelon's ABG mall, all her friends were going there as a sale of 50% sale was going on over there. Tanushree chewing the boiled veggies asked her what was the need of shopping? Dodo replied there was a cultural function at school and everyone would come with their parents.

Tanushree rudely asked her to just shut up and also reminded her about the inkling of cutting some costs on her living. Dodo was absolutely disheartened about this and quickly finished off her dinner and went to her bed by sending a text to her best friend Siya from her dial pad phone by writing how she felt bad about this. The phone beeped, Dodo quickly checked her friend suggested her to sleep and they will talk about this on class the next day. Shinjini waited until her class teacher confirmed Siya as absent while taking attendance, Shinjini actually got rid of the bad feeling in her mind and got busy with all other friends. There were two kinds of group in her school the elite class and the upper-middle class. Some times there would be some skirmish among the two groups about their class division. Teachers of her school were also biased, but Shinjini in terms of avoiding them acted like a pro. As, she would never give them any consideration. Shinjini got back home and was hell surprised to see her mom at home on a Wednesday afternoon.

Tanushree held the cushion tight and started to cry. Dodo quickly got her mom a glass of water. Tanushree gulped the glass of water all at once looked at her daughter and started telling her that she has received a demotion at her work which meant her salary was reduced by six thousand rupees. She started to panic; Dodo asked her mom about applying somewhere else where she could get a decent hike. Tanushree answered her in a distressed tone saying it will be very difficult for her to find a job giving her a hike as none of the banks would like to hire an employee who didn't switch her company for 15 years and then received a demotion. Moreover, because of serving the bank for so many years she has created a comfortable relation with her manager and her manager was very considerate about her. Dodo wanted to know more about why did this happen, her mom said she had some issued with her higher authority chairpersons. Tanushree's manager has spared Tanushree a lot of times when Dodo was young and would fall sick often at school, Tanushree would run to her school collect her from the sick room and take her to home and take the day off. All those years her manager supported her over all these unplanned leaves. They talked some more about cutting their costs from now on.

At night after dinner, they sat down to calculate with paper, pen and calculator. The end result was no more shopping randomly, no more going to movies every Sunday, all her extracurricular happenings were stopped apart from dance, but that didn't help as her tuitions were increased. Tanushree also cut some expenses on her home expenses.

Dodo was the younger sibling among her mother's side of relatives. She had her grandma, her grandpa passed away when she was in 5th grade. Her grandma was a pension holder of her husband. Dodo had an aunt who stayed abroad with her husband who was a doctor and a daughter a year younger than Dodo. Dodo also had a maternal uncle kairav who stayed with her grandma along with his wife and twin children Kaushal and Koushik, they were in their 5th grade. On that Sunday, Dodo was at her grandma's place at Garia waiting for her mother to join for lunch. Dodo's uncle and his family didn't share good bond with Tanushree so they spoke very rare. Tanushree didn't care about them she would visit her mom and spent the whole time in her mother's bedroom and leave, very rare did she visit her brother until it was very important. Dodo was waiting for her mom at her grandma's bedroom staring at the highlight of the Bengali tv serial that was on. Her grandma suggested her to call her mom and check on her that what is taking so long for her to come back. Dodo at once called her mom and the phone was picked up by her colleague Anita informed her that they were returning back from the Electro trade building when her mom felt discomfort and fainted, she was then rushed to the nearby hospital ARIS; Anita suggested to inform her grandma and immediately meet Anita at their Dhakuria house.

Dodo's grandma Shakuntala devi was an aged lady, her age was around 70, she barely walked out of her room, so Dodo didn't want to stress her upon this. Dodo informed her grandma partially and rushed to her home while leaving she heard her grandmother to yell at Kairav by saying call your sister and check she is in some trouble. Having heard that Shinjini also knew that her uncle would do nothing. Her maternal uncle's house was a flat structure house it was a 3 storey building, each floor had average 2bhk apartment size. Dodo's uncle stayed in second floor whereas Shakuntala devi used to stay in the ground floor. They had everything separated.

Shinjini finally reached home saw Anita was already waiting for her. Shinjini and Anita both entered their flat while Anita narrated everything to Shinjini, Anita asked Shinjini to search her mom's wardrobe to see where the medical insurance papers are! Shinjini was not briefed regarding this by her mom, she thought to herself that she should have asked her mom earlier what to do in this kind of situation. Finally, Shinjini got the file and on their way to the hospital she just keeps staring at the road, lost in revulsive thoughts her hunger was somehow vanished. Anita described her about the chain of events that occurred in Tanushree's life, Anita told Shinjini that Tanu would rent around 15-20 thousand from me in the month of June for your admission which she repaid me within another three months. This went on for the last 4 years. But, this year I couldn't help her because my dad had an accident I had to spend all my solid cash for him as he didn't have any Mediclaim. So, if it was about credit card I would have helped her really. After she faced demotion, she was already very tensed, I only knew that she was thinking about taking a personal loan from bank but due to some financial crunch she failed to give her home loan EMI and acknowledges a defaulter which hampers her civil score she was in some much of pain mentally as well. From morning, since I met her she looked disturbed. After the scan and rest of the preliminary tests the doctor thinks she had a cerebral attack. Anita called out Shinjini get down we have reached. Shinjini was lost in her thoughts she quickly got down from the cab and followed Anita.

45 hours passed, Anita once took Shinjini to her home forcefully in between to fed her and to freshen her up otherwise Shinjini would not move an inch from her seat at the waiting room. The doctor informed Anita that Tanushree was out of danger but her life has to be shaped in a lot of limitations. For another 1 week they will keep her in observation and then if there was no deterioration, they will release her. Anita asked Dodo

to shift to her grandma's place for a week and she assured her that she would visit her every day in the evening (visiting hours). Anita dropped Shinjini at Garia, Shinjini just carried a small backpack of clothes as she knew books won't be required as she anyways can't go to school. Shakuntala devi welcomed her and asked her to have her dinner and quickly catch some sleep. Dodo was lying next to her grandma, she clutched Shakuntala devi's dupatta lining with her fingers with her hand and started to cry. Shakuntala devi asked her to stop and sleep everything will be alright. Shakuntala devi knew that Tanushree lacked in many places as a mother as she remained more frustrated about the failures of a ideal perfect life, which she didn't have.

Within the next one week, Shakuntala devi managed to withdraw some savings for her daughter's medicine and hospital bill expenses. But she was very tensed thinking that what would happen after Tanu recovers as she won't be the same again. Shakuntala devi could barely walk so she requested Anita to visit the hospital, Anita informed her that she was at the hospital. Anita did all the formalities and showed everything to Shinjini. Shinjini realized the total bill of the hospital was 6 lakh out of which 5 lakh was provided by the Mediclaim company and the rest was given by Shakuntala devi.

Shinjini looked at her mom's face on her way back to their home. The face looked pale. Tanushree was a weak person and so looked very different from what she looked 10 days ago.

Anita visited Tanuhsree everyday at the hospital inside her cabin but Dodo didn't because she feels puckish from the smell of anesthesia and iodoform. So she practically visited the hospital every day to just snoop about Tanu in person from Anita. Shinjini reached home with Tanushree on a hot summer afternoon. Anita didn't speak much with Tanu on financial issues and welcomed her back and left early.

After Anita left Tanushree asked Dodo that how was everything managed? But Dodo remembered what Anita has trained her so she quickly told her mother that She need to rest and not stress about anything else right now.

One month passed, Dodo completely stopped going to school and take care about her mother. Tanushree had to leave her job at the bank as she couldn't do a stressful job and because she worked in the HR department she had to be really busy phones and meetings the whole day. Moreover, Tanushree was a changed person now she didn't have any energy left to tackle such things nor she had so much of physical ability left. Tanushree started a work from home job of an administrator for an abroad coaching website, she could only manage the home loan EMI and food expense for two people. Tanushree was getting better as she was able to remember a lot of past things and act accordingly but she couldn't remember recent past events. In between all these Shinjini somehow lost her track of studies as the whole day she would cook and help her mother with buying groceries and sit alone in the corner of her balcony the rest of the time. Days passed like this until one day Kairav called Tanushree and said that if she could back her the 50 thousand that Shakuntala devi has given her as he needed the money urgently before hanging up, he also added that since he provided the money in such short notice, he expects the same from his sister. Heartbroken Tanu calls Shakuntala devi, Shakuntala devi handles the situation by selling her gold bangles. Tanushree often visited Shakuntala devi as Shakuntala started to fall sick very frequently.

September, 2012.

Shakuntala devi passed away, all the rays of hope, positivity are vanished with her. Tanushree was not helped by her mother's widow pension anymore now. Even if she thought about selling her mom's part of the property then also she had to spend a lot on advocates as her brother won't let it go so easily. She can even afford the fore close charges for her own flat's home loan or sell it. Afterall, resale properly of over 15 years have less value. One day, Tanushree took a quick break from work made a coffee for herself and asked Dodo about what she was planning to do with her life and why doesn't she go to school? That's when it started to get ugly between them Dodo looked straight at her mom's eyes and said I had to discontinue because you cannot afford it. Tanushree got pissed off and said who asked you to worry? Did I ask you ? I got a brain cerebral still what has changed you are lazy that is the only reason you are not going to school. Shinjini yelled at her mom by saying oh really? If I am lazy, I would just sit at home and eat with your earnings, but I am not doing so! I am planning my ways of income out. Shinjini also reminded her mom that just because of Shakuntala devi she could somehow manage and overcome the financial crunch. Dodo left the room in disgust, though Tanu kept on shouting at her back by saying first raise your child single handedly and this is what you get in return. Dodo turned towards a Tanu and said that's the problem of parents like you who doesn't even have the financial backup to provide their child with the necessities still they plan a child, such careless parents they prove themselves as. Tanushree supposed great, go on, saying whatever you like I am sure your dad wherever he is, would be very proud of you.

For the next few weeks, they didn't talk to each other unless it was too important. Shinjini told her mom that she wants to work in event management industry. This came as a shock to her mother as she wanted her to finish her studies first but she had no choice but to stay quiet as she literally can't afford such exceeding amounts of fees for her school. Shinjini went to shopping and bought the most important four things for a girl to proceed in this field those were a white shirt, black trousers, blazer and a pair of covered shoes. Shinjini was actually guided by a school senior whose name was Debolina. Debolina was into events for more than 3 years, she did events as part-time jobs.

No later than this, Shinjini got her first event and then another and some more. This was a smooth journey for her as she rocked her job. She would look like a mini version of air hostess and talk fluently in English with all the business people around. Shinjini was never a shy girl, she always remained confident at her work. Shinjini slowly started to save money for her education as she has wasted the whole of 2012 and was looking forward to take readmission in class 9 in the upnext session. Tanushree would find it very difficult to run all the costs of her household in her little income so Shinjini started to take up some responsibilities like paying the electricity bill and pay for the Mediclaim insurance and stuffs like this. Shinjini and Devolina went for shopping at a mall in south Kolkata after their event got over that rainy evening. Both were a bit wet so they thought to wait inside the mall and also buy some dresses that they would be needing, Debolina and Shinjini both had dial pad phones so there no much access to social media back at that time. Shinjini couldn't help but noticed herself in the changing room very minutely as she felt she is growing attractive and beautiful her body was developing and she was gradually entering into her sweet sixteen. After shopping they sat in the food court and had some pizzas. Debolina asked Shinjini whether she has a boyfriend or not! Shinjini said 'no! I actually never got a chance to make one'! Debolina was not very surprised to hear this as she knew her right from childhood. Debolina actually introduced her to a guy in her friend circle whose name was Aadit. Aadit was in class 9 then, but only academically. He was atleast 4 years senior to Shinjini. Aadit was a passionate little music lover, maybe he also wanted to be a musician someday. Aadit and Shinjini exchanged no. via Debolina. Both started to talk to each other over texts and phone calls.

Shinjini was first time dating a guy so she was really impatient for taking it further. But, Aadit suggested her to slow down and just experience the old school love. Shinjini continued to work more as she only had few months to earn by doing full time work. Aadit decided to meet Shinjini after three weeks of texting and calling. Aadit usually went to gym in the morning so he decided to meet Shinjini after gym.They both met at café nearby for breakfast and had long chats about life and each other. Shinjini started to be very shy around Aadit for no good reason. She would skip to drink or have food infront of Aadit. She would maintain a distance from Aadit by keeping her funky cloth side bag in between. Aadit would enjoy all these as he knew everything was first time for Shinjini. Later, that evening Shinjini went back to home and opened her petite diary to make some calculations on expense. She managed to save one thousand after making all the payments. She decided to go shopping for herself and save the rest. Tanu called her for snacks and asked for some money for her medicines. Tanu somehow was very relaxed because Shinjini was growing into a lady, young and a responsible lady. Shinjini that night at dinner table noticed that she has been serving with the same pickle curry along side her dishes. She asked her mom 'why are you giving this everyday to me? Have you made a lot?'. Tanu replied in a low voice saying the food is mostly boiled and less spicy, so it helps to preserve the appetite. 'Great, now I have to adjust in my food habit too or starve?' Shinjini said in disgust. Tanu banged her feet on the table she shouted and asked her what is wrong with her, in every possible way she wants her to be ok. They had an ugly fight that night which made the communication between them more stiff. Shinjini never shared anything much to Aadit about her family. Once Shinjini was over phone call with Aadit when her mother suddenly enters the room. Shinjini quickly pretends as if she is talking to Debolina and the situation remains under control. Shinjini started to fall for Aadit, they would chat the whole day over text and also make phone calls and whisper to each other. While whispering, Shinjini never understood a word of Aadit's at once. But Aadit every single time would understand what Shinjini told him. Eventually they had a deal, Aadit would call her Dodo. Shinjini only came out when Aadit had to discuss anything serious to her. Aadit and Dodo met at a park for their next date, that is when Aadit proposed to her. Dodo accepted his proposal, two of them became closer and started to roam around. Snooping neighbors quickly started to notice everything and gossip among themselves, like it always happens. Dodo didn't care much about them. She only cared about her mom. Aadit took Dodo to new places, when she had free time apart from her work. Months passed like these and it was time for Dodo to take admission for 9th standard. Aadit helped her with all the paper works related to admission, while he got promoted to class 10. Dodo took admission through distance education so; she was not required to go to school every single day. This helped her to continue working at events. Dodo met a lot of boys at her work but she promised herself not to date them ever in her life for their lifestyle. Not even so-called business mans.

June,2013.

Dodo was returning from her school on her way back to home. She got a call from Aadit who asked her to meet him at their meeting point at the back gate of kitty park. Aadit had a bike, (not his own, his fathers of course) Dodo got into his bike and asked him 'hey, where are we headed to?'. Aadit asksed her to wait and eventually find out. Shinjini freezed when she saw Aadit has brought her to his home. He introduced her to his parents who were equally shocked to see her. Dodo thought to herself that this house seems to be very weird. Aadit's mother Malini welcomed her and offered her to have lunch with them. But, Malini managed to ask Aadit once that has she bunked her school! Dodo was so shy that if she had a chance she would run out of the house. They had lunch together, within next half an hour. Dodo faced a lot of difficulty while eating at their place as they were pure bangals, and Dodo as you can guess was a ghoti. For non-bengali readers, there are two types of Bengali(bongs) bangal and ghoti, these two types differ mainly in their food habits and accent. Therefore, smelly sutki and loitta were served to Dodo. Post lunch, Dodo sat down to chat with Aadit's mom who told her that Aadit had a gf called Samantha, after their breakup he has started late night returns and also alcohol.

Shinjini being furious thought how adjusting and cooperative parents Aadit has got, he should stop all these non-senses. Malini was paused as Aadit entered the room took Dodo and left the living room. He took Dodo to his brother's bedroom upstairs as there was a lovely attached balcony with it. His brother Deep stayed at Bangalore and worked for an IT firm. He would visit his family only in occasions. Dodo entered the room only to discover that the room was a total mess. Dodo looked at Aadit's face both the eyes met and they burst into laughter. They went to the balcony which had a huge field facing view, 15-19 years of boys played cricket on one side and children on the other side played football. Dodo carefully looked at the field as she realized the field was so big in size that six more groups can easily fit in the field. The summer sun kissed their face. It was a warm summer afternoon. They sat next to each other and started chatting over family. Since, Shinjini was not comfortable enough to start off, Aadit continued to speak. Shinjini got to know that Aadit had a big brother who is 9 years elder than him. He completed his MBA and started his career in 2010. He also had a high school gf who can considered to be his fiancé who's name wa Sumi. Sumi sometimes visits their house to check on them and she is a darling sister according to Aadit. Aadit's father was a garment retailer, who helped her mother Malini in all the chores of household. A loving husband and father too. And lastly, Malini who looked like a goddess, had a stroke few years back. Since then, she remains sick all the time and stressful things are kept away from her. Above all they looked like a very happy family. Shinjini opened up a little about her life to Aadit they both connected to each other on one point that they had to be mature much earlier than age because of their ailing mothers. Aadit held Shinjini's hand and took her close to his chest. Shinjini felt shy but she also felt very relaxed with the gentle touch. Shinjini thought they should kiss, so she looked up at his eyes and almost tried to kiss on his lips. But, Aadit stopped her saying 'hey, this is just a moment we had. It can wait, there is no rush'! Shinjini felt awkward and she hid her face in Aadit's chest. Then, while biding his parents' goodbye, she realized that she has become a part of their family. She was told to visit as soon as possible. Aadit came to drop her, she sprang up from his bike and in a rush asked him that 'hey, where will you go after this?'. Aadit got puzzled and replied 'will meet some friends but why?'.Shinjini held his hand strong and said 'promise me you won't drink regularly'. Aadit gave a trivial smile and said 'only occationally!'.

July,2013.

Random hangouts became very normal to Aadit and Dodo. They almost meet every single day and were very attached. Both the families knew about this, there were troubles from Tanu but that was eventually relaxed as Aadit seemed to be a very good boy to Tanu. Somehow, Tanu couldn't ask for anything else but a family like Aadit's. Tanu tried a lot to make Shinjini understand that she should equally focus on her studies, but she was easily shut by Dodo as she couldn't even bear any single private tutor of Dodo. Moreover, Shinjini earned money for her family so everything got relaxed as it always happens. Shinjini joined Aadit's gym, so in the morning they would go to gym together following Aadit's home where she would have her lunch. They would have long chats the whole evening and then Dodo would be dropped home by Aadit. When Dodo had an event or had to go to school Aadit would pickup her up from her workplace and drop her at her home. But, this routine came to an end when Aadit had to return back to her school regularly as he started to lack attendance. The duo had a pact of only meeting each other on weekends. But, this hampered Shinjini's work life balance as maximum high- budget events normally takes place in weekends. Sometimes they would start fighting on silly issues like phone recharge packs as they had to go for the cheapest connection, which got connected only when they were outside of their respective homes. The young couple struggled a lot to talk to each other.

September,2013.

Aadit and Shinjini were lying next to each other at the balcony room of Aadit's home. They were celebrating there one year anniversary. Both looked at the ceiling fan and didn't talk to each other for five minutes. They just finished having romantic cuddles as no one was at home. Aadit could barely manage to get close with her because his parents were always around. Breaking the silence Aadit asked Dodo,' why aren't you at facebook?' Dodo replied 'I don't know, never felt the need'. Aadit suggested that they should give a status of 'in a relationship' therefore Dodo should open an account in fb. The process went on and finally the account was made. Dodo looked carefully on the profile picture and asked her bf 'don't you feel this is too professional type? Like LinkedIn?' Aadit said 'no, it's not, it can be used in informal purposes like talking to friends. Talking to girlfriend'. He paused and came forward across the ThinkPad to kiss Dodo. For the celebrations, they bought four beers and crispy fried chicken. Dodo was used to liquor as she was into events, launches and promotions. One beer was down, they started to talk about feelings and occasionally would look at each other and gaze. Three beers down, they started to laugh aloud almost disturbing the yoga classes of the neighbor building. The crispy chicken came to an end, Aadit lit his cigarette and started to talk about his brother. While Dodo managed to finish few left pieces of the chicken. Aadit continued, Deep was always a brilliant student and an obedient child so he managed an MBA from the Amity University. But somehow their father had to take a lot of loans to support his son. Sumi too supported Deep at that time. Shinjini really adored how Sumi has done so much of adjustments only to be with Deep. They still had to undergo a long-distance relation. Somehow Shinjini started to forget about her dreams and herself (the very famous manufacturing defect in women, they forget to value themselves) she started to compensate her dreams for Aadit's family.

March,2014.

Aadit's board exam was over. He was super excited as there would three months of free time in his hands. Aadit somehow loved Dodo in a way that helped Dodo to get rid of all her sorrows. Tanu once invited Aadit over dinner to have a casual chat right after his boards, Shinjini prepared his favourite items for dinner.

They had a lovely dinner. Post- dinner Tanu asked Aadit what his future plan was! Aadit thought for a moment enjoys the cold breeze at terrace, then replied 'aunty I want to work as an animator.' Later that night, Shinjini and Aadit ere chatting over a facebook post about a girl. These were the non- filter generation, where good picture only meant a good phone with very less basic edit. Shinjini finds out a girl hitting on his bf, therefore she asked Aadit in every possible way that whether he was interested in her or not! They chatted a bit more and went off to sleep. Next morning, Shinjini was as ususal busy at her work in an event. Shinjini was dressed up in a pink uniform saree she looked like a smarter airhostess, she had a tea break of fifteen minute at work so she decided to call home and ask her mother to take a parcel of hers that was going to arrive that day. But Tanu didn't pickup her call. Shinjini waited for some more time and finally she gave up and joined her mates to resume work. At lunch break she again called home but there was no response. Shinjini was tensed as she had to work for another few hours but with this kind of tension in her head it was becoming rigid. Shinjini called up Aadit who just got out of his school, right after he heard about this the next moment, he headed towards Shinjini's place. The day was proved to be a bleak day for both. Tanushree always called back Shinjini in an hour or so even if she is busy at a meeting. But that day, Aadit continued to press the bell of their house only to receive no reply. Aadit informed to situation to Shinjini was rushed from her work and joined Aadit. Shinjini carried a duplicate key of their house so she managed to get inside the house only to see Tanu was lying at her bed peacefully. Tanu was faint, splash of sporadic water didn't help her to wake up! Aadit asked his father for medical contact. They succeeded in calling a medicine doctor at their place. After a checkup of twenty long minutes, he woke up Tanu by slapping on both her cheeks mildly. The doctor heard her medical history and got the detailed info on her medicines. He then turned to Aadit and said that Tanu is taking a lot of tension lately and she even took anti-depression pills. As a result, her body is reverting back. The doctor suggested Shinjini that she should look after her mom's foof habits and also to make sure she doesn't stress up. Two months from then were a tough time for both Shinjini and Aadit. Shinjini couldn't go to work or market. Tanushree suffered a lot and was taking a lot of time to recover. Tanushree's new medicines were working but slowly just as the doctor said. Doctor came in every three weeks at their home to check on her. Aadit did a few musical shows and helped her father in his shop in return of a good pocket money. He backed up Dodo in her most troubled time. Shinjini started to lose weight like never before and also started to weakened. Aadit for two whole months supplied them their food from his place. Aadit's mother always supported him when it came to Dodo. He would come in the afternoon with a packed lunchbox which also contained their dinner. This went on for some more weeks and Tanushree finally got better.

July,2014.

Dodo always stayed over a call with Aadit even if they were n ot talking it become their habit. They fought a lot over social media issue but they both believed that when the fighting night is over the next morning is meant for patch-up. Eventually, after this break it was hard for Dodo to find work with very little contacts, people working is events knows how payments are delayed from clients. That is what happened to Dodo and moreover because of leaving her last work midway she happened to be rumored unprofessional girl among her working gang. Shinjini started to give home tuition to kids of her locality. Ofcourse Dodo also did occasional events, she realized every while that she had to make more money, more money. Shinjini was growing sexier and she also choose to stay fit and well maintain herself. She realized that male attension was growing towards her like anything. Aadit's friends also started hitting on her. Aadit and Shinjini were too yng to handle such complications in life and also to deal with relationship glitches. Shinjini somehow kept on nagging her bf. This started to make the relationship more toxic. Sometimes Dodo would talk to any of his friend in an over-friendly way, the next moment Aadit will take the revenge by texting his ex. Apart from all of the above they still loved each and other. Both of them had their own share points. Aadit would share everything to his brother Deep. And Dodo would share everything to Arup (her fb friend, who was way senior to her but the duo still liked to share everything to each other). Shinjini would often visit Aadit and have private moments at his bedroom. Shinjiini even after being with him, remained a virgin. Somehow, she was too scared to even open up to her own bf. She had strange type of panic when she was approached for making love. But, Aadit was an extra moderate person who always treated Dodo with love and care. He never rushed and gave his best. Shinjini and Aadit became busy with their exam and work altogether, by then they found a pattern for themselves and their love life. Deep returned back to kol, so as a result random visit of Sumi increased. Shinjini too visited and quickly realized that Sumi somehow didn't appreciate Shinjini at all. Shinjini knew that Deep and Sumi encouraged Samantha way better. Well frankly this was a real issue of fighting between Aadit and Dodo as in that phase they didn't know how to avoid or deal with lethal people.

Sept,2014,

Kolkata was having a typical monsoon month. Shinjini was wrapped with her blanket and on a call with Aadit. Aadit asked her to come over as the whole family were supposed to go at a relative's place and they can be home alone for some hours. Both of them were excited and having a chance didn't want to miss it. There was a typical place at Aadit's balcony room when Aadit would make Dodo wait for long hours when it was not the right time to come out. Dodo had excellent hiding skills therefore. Aadit managed to hid Dodo in presence of his family who were busy for getting ready. Now, Dodo was asked to wait in silence, Malini asked Aadit to drop her and Deep in the first place and then to lock the house and to join with his father.

Aadit came closer to that closet type store room and told Dodo to wait for fifteen minutes and he will come back. Shinjini knew very well his fifteen minutes meant fourty five minutes but helplessly smiled. Dodo had all arrangements to survive over there she had earlier set a pillow over there kept room freshener and carried both food and water. She quickly thought to fall in a power nap. Lying there she knew there were no one in this house and only in few more minutes she is going to have a lovely time. She was lost in her thoughts when she heard the door opening sound of that room. She was hell nervous as she knew that it was not Aadit, then who was it? Shinjini knowas that Aadit's arrival would mean his bike sound first. Shinjini was much embarrassed already so thought what should her response be. She heard footsteps but couldn't understand who it was, before she could think any further Aadit's father Shaymol opened the closet and saw Shinjini. Shinjini felt mortified like never before. Shaymol didn't seem to be surprised at all. He asked Dodo why are you hiding over hear? This is my house you can always come here with you head dangled up. Why are you hiding. He asked Shinjini to follow him to the balcony. Shinjini always knew Aadit's father preferred Shinjinji over sumi, but Malini preferred Sumi over Shinjini. But there was a feeling of discomfiture and fear altogether for Shinjini. Shaymol went back to his bedroom and closed the door of the balcony, he chatted a lot with Dodo and Dodo didn't feel anything fishy and chatted some more. Shaymol closed the connecting door of the room and asked Shinjini to sit with him at the bed. That's when Dodo started to feel weird. But she still managed to sit at a distance. Shaymol sensed it and quickly asked her about her future plans, she then anxiously replied I want to be a sports journalist. Shaymol smiled and said but I think you will be great at business. You can manage my shop. Dodo smiled a bit but thought to herself sometimes when Aadit dropped her Shaymol would also sit behind her and come half a way. Aadit sometimes triple carried and droped his father to market. In such moments, Shaymol would place his head sidewise on her back. This eventually made her uncomfortable but she didn't pay much attention to it. Shaymol aked Dodo where was she lost? But, Shinjini quickly sprang up the bed and said I need to leave, I will meet Aadit afterwards. She didn't listen to whatever Shaymol had to say and rushed towards the stairs, but she was caught by Shaymol from back even before she could do anything Shaymol started assailing her. She violently pushed him out and escaped the house even without wearing shoes. She met Aadit right out side of the house. Aadit tried to calm her but failed. Aadit shouted and asked what was wrong but Dodo in absolute panic only said 'he tried to...'.

Shinjini returned home ran to her mom, but she couldn't share anything. Later that night, Shinjini picked up his call and shared the whole thing after few hesitations. Aadit informed her about his father's character history of being a loose-character person.

But, Aadit told her that he had never heard anything in the last eight years though. Then, Aadit said 'Samantha and Sumi have never faced any such issue'. Before the situation got worst, Aadit managed the whole situation by calming her down. The next morning, Aadit went to Shinjini's house and asked for a little help. He said that its hard to let people know without any proof, you have to make a video with him where his activity needs to be captured. Dodo asked Aadit whether he was drunk, as he was talking like a dork! Aadit convinced Shinjini after three weeks of pleading, Shinjini went to Aadit's house only to hear from Malini that why don't you come over, are you guys again fighting and stuff. Shinjini didn't pay attention to any of these and managed to get Shaymol alone in kitchen.

Shaymol thought Shinjini to be very easy thus came closer and strted touching her, somehow, he had a shade confidence on himself. It sucked, it just sucked for Shinjini but as the situation demanded she managed to take a video.

November,2014.

A month has passed, Dodo and Aadit were not in touch. The month of October is supposed to be the festive month of Kolkata, it lights up like a bride, the arrival of Durga maa makes all of the city happy! But, in the month of October Aadit and Shinjini were busy to prove themselves. Aadit showed the video to his mom, Sumi and Deep. It came as a shock to the family and thus all of them suggested Aadit to leave Shinjini, as they believed such a bitch would only bring miseries to the family. Deep even called up Shinjini to say 'Do you want to ruin our happy family? If not, leave! Just leave!' Aadit was forced by her family, blackmailed by her mom to cut contact with Shinjini. Shinjini one day got pissed off and even called up Arup for some help, Arup saw the video and said 'police could only help if you restricted him and questioned him! This video is showing a mutual consent, why didn't you prevent him Dodo?'

Dodo remained silent and said 'Aadit asked me not to prevent so that he can show his family what a pervert his father is.'

silence

1964 Chinsurah,

I gave birth to a pre-mature child at early seven months of pregnancy. I was told that my child is not completely healthy but will survive though, shocking, isn't it?

Yes, these things are very common in a government hospital in wb. Back then these things seemed normal even to the nurses to inform the new mom about all the complexities. Yes, there I was lying with shields of blood, filthy smell and horror.

1962 Chinsurah,

I was eldest daughter of my parents, along with five siblings. I got married first in my family; I was the eighth generation of the Sen's. A lot of bongs must have heard about Gouri sen{legendary bong}, he was remembered for giving away money to poor people, rest I suggest you to google ;]

My name is Krishna , so being the eldest daughter my duty was to free my parents as soon as I turn 18 as that would be better from them on so many levels. I often received proposals from my entire neighborhood, that defines my outer appearance, I had large dark eyes, and waist length thick black hair. But as the name suggests my complexion was dark. My whole childhood was ruined only on this tension that how am I supposed to get married. Honestly, I didn't' care at all! All I cared about was my studies and my singing. Uh! Did I tell you, just to stop both of these my mother arranges a normal looking captivity for 4 years till the time I turned 18. My father was the only person in the whole who probably had feelings for me, he usually went for business trips when my mother used to look me. I have had enough before marriage, enough.

The year I turned 18 my father came home to give a surprise visit only to discover his daughter lying on the ground with dirty clothes on and looking pale. He then decides to marry me off. He could not think of anything else as this would mean keeping me away from my mother's evil eye. So, yea, I got married to a gentle looking guy. On my marriage night I discovered that my husband Santosh works for a nationalized bank. The whole night was filled with cheerful chats, getting to know each other conversations. The next day though I realized what a hell I had landed in! Santosh always took my side on all the hardships and saas-bahu episodes I have had in my entire 8 years of stay over there but I merely had any support about our children, yes! My first child born after 2 years of my marriage, a pre-mature handicapped baby. He had glitter in his eyes, my ultimate joy was clearly in my arms. After two years of my first child my second child born my younger daughter. Life has been a roller coaster since my first pregnancy, I was not given enough food at my in-law's home, husband having a decent salary had to give away everything to his parents as there were loans on their head after this marriage. I was asked to even wash clothes on my final months. My father tried several times to bring me back at their parental home but they did not allow it either. Lastly, my father only sent dozens of high calcium and high protein foods, which never reached me!

After 7 years of marriage, I understood my son wont ever talk or hear any sound but my daughter whom I wanted to abort was completely normal. After the doctor[SP1] suggested us a better treatment

We decided to move to uttarpara, a 3-storey house is what my husband gifted me on our 8th anniversary. My best years of life was at uttarpara for 35 years.

My glowing days,

Uttarpara 1970,

My father could now visit me freely as there were no boundaries set for him now, my struggle started from the day we shifted as I had to take my son to Kolkata for his voice therapy classes while leaving my daughter behind. No mobile phones or landline was available then, random surprise visit from neighbors and relatives often meant I will sleep hungry. Did I tell you it was worst in the first couple of years financially but I was still happy because we were at peace. After 17 years of daily travel to kol, my son finally said his first words to me saying "ma"..

That moment it was all worth it, but if God gave me something he also snatched something in return. My daughter grown up to be a stubborn quitted her studies in class11 and never pursued them back. She eventually got married at 25. I never was at peace with either of my daughter nor with son-in-law. They robbed my emotions and something more than that too! After a miscarriage, she was blessed with 2 healthy sons. Here ends her chapter.

My son got divorced after 5 years of her marriage and we got drained away financially. I then had to bring up my granddaughter as both my son and daughter-in-law would never do their duties.

My husband passed away when my granddaughter was in class 6, leaving me only our 3 storey house. Well, let's just say she is happily married to her love of life, she is a successful entrepreneur and also a language trainer. My son is with me, though he was never a good father he has passed as a good son!